PARENTS AND CAREGIVERS,

Stone Arch Readers are designed to provide enjoyable reading experiences, as well as opportunities to develop vocabulary, literacy skills, and comprehension. Here are a few ways to support your beginning reader:

- Talk with your child about the ideas addressed in the story.

- Discuss each illustration, mentioning the characters, where they are, and what they are doing.

- Read with expression, pointing to each word. You may want to read the whole story through and then revisit parts of the story to ensure that the meanings of words or phrases are understood.

- Talk about why the character did what he or she did and what your child would do in that situation.

- Help your child connect with characters and events in the story.

Remember, reading with your child should be fun, not forced. Each moment spent reading with your child is a priceless investment in his or her literacy life.

GAIL SAUNDERS-SMITH, PH.D.

STONE ARCH **READERS**

are published by Stone Arch Books
151 Good Counsel Drive, P.O. Box 669
Mankato, Minnesota 56002
www.stonearchbooks.com

Library of Congress
Cataloging-in-Publication Data
Meister, Cari.
   Three Claws, the mountain monster /
by Cari Meister; illustrated by Dennis Messner.
   p. cm. – (Stone Arch readers)
   ISBN 978-1-4342-1633-5 (library binding)
   ISBN 978-1-4342-1748-6 (paperback)
   [1. Bad breath–Fiction. 2. Monsters–Fiction.]
I. Messner, Dennis, ill. II. Title.
PZ7.M515916Thr 2010
[E]–dc22   2009000890

Summary: Three Claws has
bad breath, which bothers
the other monsters.

Creative Director: Heather Kindseth
Designer: Bob Lentz

Reading Consultants:
Gail Saunders-Smith, Ph.D.
Melinda Melton Crow, M.Ed.
Laurie K. Holland, Media Specialist

Printed in the United States of America

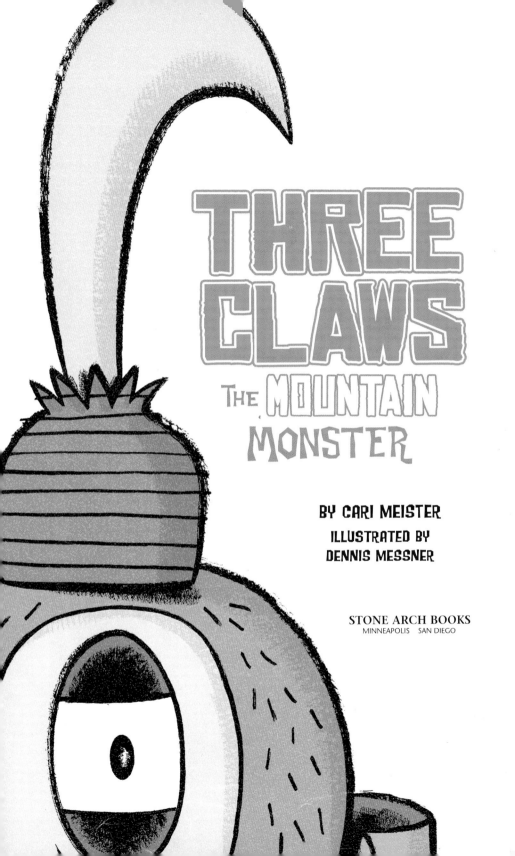

THREE CLAWS
THE MOUNTAIN MONSTER

BY CARI MEISTER

ILLUSTRATED BY
DENNIS MESSNER

STONE ARCH BOOKS
MINNEAPOLIS   SAN DIEGO

THREE CLAWS

This is Three Claws. He
has one big eye. He has two
furry legs.

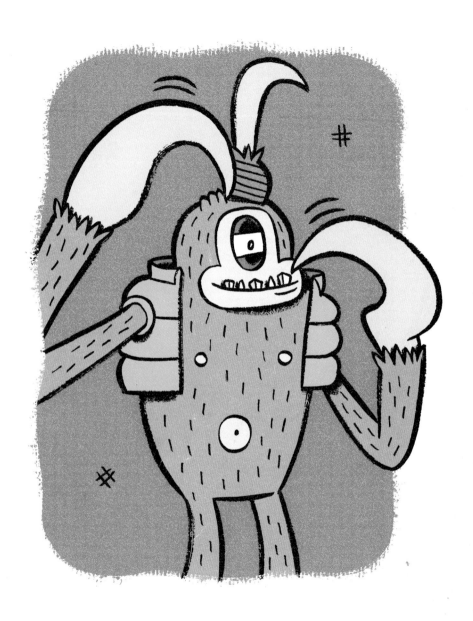

He has three sharp claws.

The claw on his head is
handy. He uses it to catch fish.

He uses it to climb icy
mountains.

He even uses it to do cool tricks.

Three Claws is very cool.
Everybody thinks so.

But Three Claws has one big problem.

He has bad breath. He has
really, really bad breath.

His favorite food is rotten fish.

The mountain monsters want him to eat other things.

They make the best monster food.

None of these foods stink. They smell good.

The mountain monsters invite
Three Claws to a big feast.

There are trays of food.

There are baskets of food.

There are even foods hopping on the floor.

"Try this," the monsters say.

"Try that," the monsters say.

"No, thank you," says Three
Claws. "I only eat rotten fish.
Would you like some?"

The mountain monsters
shake their heads. They groan.

What are they going to do
with Three Claws?

21

The mountain monsters have a meeting. They like Three Claws, but he is too smelly.

What can they do?

One of the monsters points to the top of the mountain. "We need someone to live up there," says the monster.

"We need someone to watch over our mountain. We need someone to tell us when people come hunting for us," he says.

"Three Claws has a big eye. He can see better than any of us. His breath will scare people away. We will not smell him from way up there," says another monster.

The monsters clap. The monsters cheer. It is a great idea.

The next day, the monsters
come to Three Claws.

"Three Claws, your one eye
can see better than any other
monster eye. Will you watch
over the mountain for us?"
they ask.

Three Claws drops his fish.
He blinks his eye. He bows
down low.

"Yes," he says. "It would be
a great honor."

Three Claws climbs to the top of the mountain. It is cold. It is quiet. It is lonely.

Then Three Claws unpacks a
few of his favorite things. There!
Now it smells like home.

THE END

STORY WORDS

mountain　　smelly

everybody　　cheer

breath　　blinks

favorite

Total Word Count: 362

MEET ALL FOUR OF OUR MONSTERS!